# Baa-rmy Drawing Book

First Published in Great Britain 2007
by Egmont UK Limited
239 Kensington High Street, London W8 6SA

© and ™ Aardman Animations Ltd. 2007. All rights reserved.
Shaun the Sheep (word mark) and the character 'Shaun the Sheep' © and ™ Aardman Animations Limited.
Based upon an idea by Nick Park.
Developed by Richard (Golly) Goleszowski with Alison Snowden and David Fine.

ISBN 978 1 4052 3360 6
3 5 7 9 10 8 6 4 2
Printed in Italy by Rotolito Lombarda

All rights reserved. No part of this publication may be reproduced, stored
in a retrieval system, or transmitted, in any form or by any means, electronic,
mechanical, photocopying, recording or otherwise, without the prior
permission of the publisher and copyright owner.

D0316533

# Here comes Shaun the Sheep!
# But where are the rest of the flock?
# Can you draw lots of sheep behind Shaun?

# The sheep are pulling funny faces! Draw what you think they look like on these blank faces.

# It's time for a bath! Draw the sheep having fun in the sheep dip as Shaun jumps in.

# What do you think Shaun is aiming at with his catapult? Draw it in the picture.

# Shirley is off to a fancy dress party.
# What do you think she is wearing?

Shaun and Timmy are throwing water balloons at a pig. Can you draw in the naughty sheep?

**Bitzer is dreaming of being on holiday. Draw where you think Bitzer wants to go in the dream bubble.**

# Shaun has decided to have a go at skiing.
# Can you draw his skis and woolly hat for him?

# Shaun has taken a photograph of all his friends. Draw it in this frame.

The pigs have been stealing the farmer's apples.
Finish this wanted poster by drawing a picture
of the apple-munching pigs.

# WANTED
## FOR APPLE MUNCHING

**REWARD: EXTRA HAY**

**The farmer is puzzled at what he's just found!
Shaun and the other sheep have left him
a smelly present. Can you draw it?**

# The sheep have built Timmy a climbing frame from things they found in the farmer's house.
# Draw what you think it looks like.

# Who do you think is standing at the top of this sheep tower?

# DJ Shaun loves spinning the vinyl.
# What do you think this record cover looks like?

# Someone poured hair dye in the sheep dip!
# What funny colours have the sheep been dyed?

# Bitzer has lost all the sheep.
# Draw where they are hiding.

# Shaun and Bitzer are playing a game of football.
## Finish the picture by adding Bitzer.

# Shaun is flying his kite. The other sheep have made kites, too. What do you think they look like?

# Uh-oh! The pigs are armed and dangerous!
# Can you draw Shaun and the flock running away?

# Timmy's mum has just told Shaun a secret.
## Draw what you think it is.

# Shaun is trying to make Timmy laugh.
# Draw what you think Shaun is doing.

# Shaun is getting into some groovy disco dancing. Can you draw the other sheep joining in?

# Timmy's mum is telling him a bedtime story. Draw the story in the panels and tell it in your own words.

Shaun thinks the farmer's tractor needs to look a bit cooler. Can you give him a hand?

# Shaun's football team needs a kit!
## Can you design one for them?

What do you think has scared little Timmy? Was it a monster? Or a ghost? Or was it the naughty pigs?

# Can you draw Shaun as a cool DJ?
## He'll need ear phones and lots of records to play.

# What do you think has happened in this news story?
## Draw the picture to go with the headline.

**EWES OF THE WORLD**

Inside today:
Grass Recipes
What's big in fleece this year
Top 10 tips for decorating your barn

# SHEEP MEETS ALIEN!

# Who do you think is hiding in the farmer's tractor?

# The greedy pigs have stolen Bitzer's picnic!
# Draw Bitzer some yummy food to replace it.

# Shaun has arranged the sheep into a pyramid.
# What do you think they look like?